The Boxcar Children Mysteries

The Boxcar Children
Surprise Island
The Yellow House Mystery
Mystery Ranch
Mike's Mystery
Blue Bay Mystery
The Woodshed Mystery
The Lighthouse Mystery
Mountain Top Mystery
Schoolhouse Mystery
Caboose Mystery
Houseboat Mystery
Snowbound Mystery
Tree House Mystery
Bicycle Mystery
Mystery in the Sand
Mystery Behind the Wall
Bus Station Mystery
Benny Uncovers a Mystery
The Haunted Cabin Mystery
The Deserted Library Mystery
The Animal Shelter Mystery
The Old Motel Mystery
The Mystery of the Hidden
  Painting
The Amusement Park Mystery
The Mystery of the Mixed-Up Zoo
The Camp-Out Mystery
The Mystery Girl
The Mystery Cruise
The Disappearing Friend Mystery
The Mystery of the Singing Ghost
Mystery in the Snow
The Pizza Mystery
The Mystery Horse
The Mystery at the Dog Show
The Castle Mystery
The Mystery of the Lost Village
The Mystery on the Ice
The Mystery of the Purple Pool
The Ghost Ship Mystery

The Mystery in Washington, DC
The Canoe Trip Mystery
The Mystery of the Hidden Beach
The Mystery of the Missing Cat
The Mystery at Snowflake Inn
The Mystery on Stage
The Dinosaur Mystery
The Mystery of the Stolen Music
The Mystery at the Ball Park
The Chocolate Sundae Mystery
The Mystery of the Hot
  Air Balloon
The Mystery Bookstore
The Pilgrim Village Mystery
The Mystery of the Stolen
  Boxcar
The Mystery in the Cave
The Mystery on the Train
The Mystery at the Fair
The Mystery of the Lost Mine
The Guide Dog Mystery
The Hurricane Mystery
The Pet Shop Mystery
The Mystery of the Secret Message
The Firehouse Mystery
The Mystery in San Francisco
The Niagara Falls Mystery
The Mystery at the Alamo
The Outer Space Mystery
The Soccer Mystery
The Mystery in the Old Attic
The Growling Bear Mystery
The Mystery of the Lake Monster
The Mystery at Peacock Hall
The Windy City Mystery
The Black Pearl Mystery
The Cereal Box Mystery
The Panther Mystery
The Mystery of the Queen's Jewels
The Stolen Sword Mystery
The Basketball Mystery

The Boxcar Children Mysteries

THE RETURN OF THE GRAVEYARD GHOST

created by
GERTRUDE CHANDLER WARNER

ALBERT WHITMAN & Company
Chicago, Illinois

Library of Congress Cataloging-in-Publication Data
is available from the publisher.

The Return of the Graveyard Ghost
Created by Gertrude Chandler Warner

ISBN 978-0-8075-6935-1 (hardcover)
ISBN 978-0-8075-6936-8 (paperback)

10 9 8 7 6 5 4 3 2 1 LB 18 17 16 15 14 13

Cover art copyright © 2013 by Tim Jessell.
Interior illustrations by Anthony VanArsdale.

For more information about Albert Whitman & Company,
visit our web site at www.albertwhitman.com.

Contents

THE RETURN OF THE GRAVEYARD GHOST

CHAPTER 1

In the Cemetery

"I think it's going to rain," twelve-year-old Jessie Alden told her younger brother, Benny. "We need to walk faster if we're going to beat the storm," she said. Jessie gently tugged on Watch's leash. The wire-haired terrier trotted between Benny and Jessie, keeping pace with their quick steps.

"I'm going as fast as I can," Benny replied. "The wind keeps pushing me backward." He looked ahead toward his ten-year-old sister, Violet, and fourteen-year-old brother,

Henry. Violet was struggling with the zipper on her jacket and Henry's hat kept flying away in the strong gusts.

"It's too cold," Henry complained as he swooped his hat off the ground for the fifth time and set it firmly over his short brown hair. "Taking Watch for a walk seemed like a good idea an hour ago—"

"It was warmer then," Violet responded with a shiver. Her two high pigtails whipped back in the wind. She gave up on the zipper and wrapped the jacket around her instead. "We should have stayed closer to home." Violet shoved her hands into her pockets.

"Nothing to do about it now," Jessie said as she and Benny caught up with their siblings.

Benny was breathing heavily. "This is crazy strong wind. If you tied a string to me, I'd be a six-year-old kite."

Jessie took Benny's hand in hers and squeezed it tight. "I'll make sure you don't blow away," she said, holding him firmly.

"I have an idea." Henry pointed to the nearby gate of the Greenfield Cemetery. "There's a shortcut this way."

"Shortcut?" Benny stared past the tall, ornate iron gate toward the moss-covered tombstones. "Sounds good to me. Let's go!" He rushed forward.

"Hang on." Jessie put a hand on Benny's shoulder. "Cemeteries are spooky." Jessie was very brave, but she was also cautious. "Are you *sure* it's okay with you, Benny?"

"I'm not a chicken." Benny put his hands on his hips. "I don't believe in ghosts."

"Once we get to Main Street, we can stop at a shop and call Grandfather for a ride," Henry told them.

"The quicker we get home, the faster we can eat!" At that, Benny's stomach rumbled. "My tummy says it's almost dinner time."

"It's only four o'clock," Henry told Benny after checking his watch.

"Hmmm." Benny pat his belly. "Feels like dinner time. My tummy needs a snack."

"You *always* need a snack!" Henry laughed.

Jessie looked to Violet. Violet often kept quiet about things. Jessie wanted to make sure Violet got a vote before they decided to go through the graveyard.

"Are you scared, Violet?" Jessie asked.

"A little," Violet admitted. "I don't know if I believe in ghosts or not. Sometimes I do. Sometimes I don't..." Violet's voice tapered off. "I suppose if everyone else wants to go that way, it's all right."

"Great!" Benny pushed open the gate. "We all agree. Come on."

Jessie held Watch's leash as they stepped onto the cobblestone path. The sky grew darker with each step they took. Violet moved close to Jessie.

Henry walked ahead with Benny. They were checking out the gravestones, taking turns reading the names and dates out loud.

Greenfield Cemetery was built on a hillside. The wind howled through a thick grove of trees planted in the oldest section. Tombstones in that part dated as far back as the late 1700s.

"There's a lot of history around us," Jessie remarked.

Benny pointed at a tombstone. He sounded out the engraved word. "Soldier."

"The soldier died in 1781. That means he probably fought in the American Revolution," Henry told Benny. "I'll read you a book about the war when we get to the house."

Jessie, Violet, Henry, and Benny lived with their grandfather. After their parents died, they ran away and hid in a railroad boxcar in the woods. They had heard that Grandfather Alden was mean. Even thought they'd never met him, they were afraid. But when he finally found the children, they discovered he wasn't mean at all. Now the children lived with him, and their boxcar was a clubhouse in the backyard.

Watch was the stray dog they'd found on their adventures.

As the first drops of rain began to fall in the cemetery, Watch barked toward a far-off building. It was along another stone pathway past the trees.

"Is that a house?" Benny asked, squinting his eyes. Drops of rain speckled his thick dark-brown hair.

"I think that's the main office," Henry replied, tilting his head to study a squat, brown building. "There's a sign out front. I can't read it, but there's also a parking lot. That's a good clue it's where Mrs. Radcliffe works."

Mrs. Radcliffe was the caretaker of the cemetery. The children had only met her once when they were out with Grandfather. Grandfather Alden had been born in Greenfield and knew practically everyone.

"You're looking the wrong way." Benny tugged on Henry's arm and pointed to the right. He asked again, "I meant is *that* a house?"

Not very far away, tucked among the gravestones, stood a stone structure, much taller than anything else. It was made of white marble, with carved columns and a triangle roof. The building looked like an ancient Greek temple. Several bouquets of white lilies were lying on the front steps.

"It's not a house," Jessie told Benny. "That's called a mausoleum."

"Maus-a-what?" Benny asked.

Violet began to explain. "It's a fancy kind of grave where—" She was about to tell Benny more, when suddenly, lightning flashed. In the glow, the children saw something move by the mausoleum. "Who's that?" Violet asked.

A shadowy figure emerged from behind the building. It was impossible to tell if it was a man or a woman. Whoever it was had on a black jacket with a hood and was moving fast around the tombstones.

The figure stopped and stood near the big mausoleum. An instant later, a flash of lightning zigzagged across the sky and the figure disappeared.

Watch snarled.

Benny stepped back and put a hand on Watch's head. "Watch is scared," he said, leaning in toward the dog. "He thinks we saw a ghost."

Jessie looked at the nervous expression on Benny's face and said, "We should get out of here."

There was a small wall around the back of the mausoleum. They could easily jump over it. Just past that was a café where they could warm up and wait for Grandfather.

Watch barked as the rain began to pour down in heavy sheets. Thunder rattled soon after the lightning.

As the children began to run, Henry glanced back over his shoulder. "Odd," he mumbled, staring at the spot where the cloaked figure had disappeared. "Something strange is going on in Greenfield Cemetery."

CHAPTER 2

The Greenfield Ghost

Randy's Café was packed with people who had also been caught in the rain. Mr. Randy was standing by the front door, handing out towels and helping hang up jackets.

While Violet called Grandfather to let him know where they were, Henry and Benny searched for seats.

Jessie crossed the café to say hello to a girl she knew.

"Hi, Vita." Jessie pointed at the camera in Vita Gupta's hand. "Out taking pictures of the storm?" Vita's nature photos were blue ribbon prizewinners.

"No. I'm changing focus," Vita said. Her short dark hair shook when she giggled at her own pun. "I'm going to make a movie instead of taking pictures. Miss Wolfson asked me to help make a short film about Greenfield using old photographs from the historical society." Vita indicated the older woman at the table and asked Jessie, "Do you know Martha Wolfson?"

"Of course," Jessie said. She turned to Miss Wolfson. "Hello," Jessie greeted her. "Nice to see you again."

"I met Jessie when she came to visit me at the historical society last summer," Miss Wolfson told Vita. She smoothed some loose strands from her gray hair into her bun with one hand. "Jessie interviewed me for a project about old buildings in Greenfield." Looking around, Miss Wolfson asked, "Is Watch with you?" She smiled. "He's a wonderful dog."

"Watch is over there with Benny and Henry." Jessie pointed to her brothers. "They're looking for a place where we can all sit together. Mr. Randy was very nice to let Watch come into the café during this rainstorm."

"You can join us," Vita said. There were three empty places at the table and something dark on the fourth seat. It was Miss Wolfson's jacket, lying out to dry.

"Hang my jacket on the hook behind you," Miss Wolfson told Jessie. "Then there will be plenty of room for you all." She pointed at an empty spot on the floor near her feet and smiled. "Watch can sit by me. I'll pet him."

Jessie set the jacket on a hook near a large, rain-splattered and steamy window. She waved to get Henry's attention.

Benny came to the table and eyed Miss Wolfson's cookie with a tilted grin.

"Would you like half?" Miss Wolfson asked.

Benny's eyes lit up. "Oh yes, thank you!" he said. He waited patiently as she broke the cookie then ate his half quickly.

Miss Wolfson chuckled and gave Benny the other piece, saying, "Don't spoil your dinner."

"Don't worry," Violet assured her. "Benny's stomach is never full."

Miss Wolfson laughed again.

"Would you like to see a few of the photographs Vita and I have selected for the film so far?" Miss Wolfson brought out a stack of pictures from her purse.

"I love old pictures." Henry leaned in closer. All the photographs were in black and white. There was one of Greenfield Elementary School, back when it was in a one-room building. There were ten students with a teacher standing in front.

Violet pointed at one of the girls in the picture. "She looks familiar." Violet glanced up at Miss Wolfson. "Is that you?"

Miss Wolfson laughed. "Goodness, no. This was taken before I was born," she told Violet. "But you made a good guess...That's my mom."

"Your mom!" Benny exclaimed. "She's so little."

"She was about your age when this picture was taken," Miss Wolfson told him. She smiled. "Mom's a whole lot older now."

Benny chuckled.

Jessie pointed at another girl about the same age wearing an old-fashioned dress. "Who's that?"

"Patty Wilson," Miss Wolfson said. "She was my mom's best friend." Miss Wolfson pulled out a different picture taken when Patty was in high school. Her blond hair was tucked under a sleek hat and she was wearing a ruffled skirt.

Patty Wilson was standing in front of a dress shop on Main Street. "Patty worked at Madame LaFonte's Dress Shop. It was the fanciest store in town."

Miss Wolfson put that photograph away and showed Violet another one. "This is Greenfield Children's Hospital," she said, "taken right after it opened, almost a hundred years ago."

"I like that picture the best," Vita said. "Did you know Miss Wolfson volunteers at the new hospital building and donates money to families with sick children?" she asked Jessie.

"That's very nice of you," Jessie told Miss Wolfson.

Miss Wolfson said, "It's a worthy cause."

"I think we should put the hospital images on the movie poster," Vita said. "I'd like to print the two pictures side by side; this one from then and a new one to show what the building looks like now. We can sell the posters to help the hospital raise money."

"The hospital always needs money," Miss Wolfson said, considering it. "I do what I can to help, but it's never enough."

"I'll add music to the movie," Vita said. "And we can interview families about the hospital."

While Vita and Miss Wolfson talked about the hospital pictures, Henry handed Jessie another old photograph. This one was of the cemetery's front gate. It was taken so many years earlier hardly any moss was growing on the tombstones. With the sun shining, the cemetery looked like a beautiful park, not a scary place for ghosts to lurk.

"There was someone spooky in the cemetery today." Benny told Miss Wolfson about the figure they'd seen. "They were by the moose-e-lum," he said.

"*Mausoleum*, you mean?" Miss Wolfson asked, raising an eyebrow.

"I don't think it was a ghost," Jessie said. "There were flowers on the steps. I've been thinking that whoever we saw probably was there to leave the bouquets."

"Hmm." Miss Wolfson pressed her lips together. "The LaFonte family had that monument specially built." She glanced away from Benny toward the window. "But there are no LaFonte family members left in Greenfield. I don't know who might have left flowers—" She paused to consider. "You know, some people say the cemetery is haunted."

"Really?" Violet's eyes widened.

"I don't believe in ghosts," Benny told Miss Wolfson. "Watch was scared though."

"Is that so?" Miss Wolfson asked, glancing down at the terrier.

The door to the café burst open with the wind. A young man wearing a black jacket and hood was standing in the doorway.

After a long look around at the faces in the shop, the boy marched over to Miss Wolfson and introduced himself. "I'm Marcus Michelson," he said. "I'm a new student at the university. Are you Miss Wolfson?"

"I am," she said.

Benny stood and let Marcus have his place. He sat back down, sharing the edge of Violet's seat.

"I think Marcus is the figure we saw in the cemetery," Henry whispered to Jessie. "He's the right height and he has the right color jacket."

"I'm interested in Greenfield history," Marcus Michelson told Miss Wolfson. He pushed back his coat's hood to reveal short blond hair.

"Is that why you were in the cemetery?" Henry interrupted. Marcus turned to face him. "We saw you standing by the LaFonte mausoleum."

"It couldn't have been me. I never went into the cemetery," Marcus insisted. His green eyes grew wide. "I was outside the gate when I saw a strange figure all dressed in black. I thought it was very suspicious, so I followed—" He looked around the coffee shop. "I was certain whoever it was ducked in here." Marcus shook his head. "I looked around but didn't see anyone who might fit the description. Then

I noticed Miss Wolfson." He caught her eye and said, "I've been meaning to call you."

"How can I help you?" Mrs. Wolfson asked.

"Well, I—" Marcus began when suddenly the lights in the coffee shop flickered off. The room plunged into darkness.

Watch jumped onto Jessie's lap.

Benny gave Violet a hug and whispered, "Don't worry. I'll protect you."

"I'll protect you too," Violet said, hugging him back.

When the lights came back on a few moments later, a woman screamed.

Her husband, pale and shaken, pointed to the window behind Henry's head.

A single lily lay across the windowsill. The raindrops on the window glittered on the glass, making the flower shine eerily.

Vita pressed a button on her camera. "Scoot over, please, Jessie," she said, holding the lens to her eye. "I want to record this."

"What's going on?" Jessie asked Miss Wolfson.

Miss Wolfson stared at the flower. She studied the frightened faces of the people in the café. Then she looked directly into the lens of Vita's camera and announced, "The LaFonte ghost has returned."

CHAPTER 3

The LaFonte Mausoleum

"Who's the LaFonte ghost?" Henry asked Miss Wolfson.

"A g-g-ghost?" Benny asked. "There's a real ghost in Greenfield?"

"I thought you didn't believe in ghosts," Jessie said.

Benny raised his shoulders. "That was before we saw something in the cemetery and the lights went out and...that!" He pointed at the flower. "I've changed my mind." Benny shivered and whispered in Watch's ear,

21

"Ghosts. Yikes."

People in the café gathered around Miss Wolfson as she began to share a bit of history.

"Today is the seventy-fifth anniversary of the death of Madame Jacqueline LaFonte," she told the crowd.

"She was the dressmaker." Jessie picked up the historic photograph of the LaFonte shop on Main Street.

"Yes." Miss Wolfson went on, saying, "Women would come to have dresses made, then stay for tea and conversation." With a small smile she added, "Madame LaFonte was known to give very good advice. Some people even say Jacqueline was a fortune-teller."

"Very interesting," Jessie said, setting the photo on the table and taking a notebook out of her small purse. Jessie wrote down Madame Jacqueline LaFonte's name as a reminder to see if she could find any information about her online. Jessie liked to research interesting people.

"Ever since the first anniversary of her death, people in Greenfield have believed that Jacqueline LaFonte's ghost haunts the cemetery," Miss Wolfson said.

"Ooh," Vita said, recording the café conversation. "A ghost story is way more interesting than a historical society film." She stood on a chair to get a good view of the room through her camera. She focused her lens on the most frightened expressions.

The door to the café opened and Grandfather

Alden walked in. "Looks like I'm interrupting an important meeting," he remarked as he closed his umbrella. He walked over to Henry and asked, "What's going on?"

Henry pointed to the windowsill.

"Ah," Grandfather said, stepping over to Miss Wolfson. "It's the three-day warning?"

The historian nodded.

At Jessie's questioning look, Grandfather explained, "Every year around Halloween, white lilies are placed on the LaFonte grave. After that, a lily appears somewhere in town. It's said that lilies were Jacqueline LaFonte's favorite flower. But some people also believe that lilies are a symbol of death." Grandfather said.

He continued. "After the flower shows up, everyone has three days to bring gifts to the LaFonte mausoleum. Those who leave gifts get a year of good fortune. Those who ignore the warning receive nothing but bad luck all year."

Miss Wolfson clarified. "Gifts can be food, silver, money, jewelry—anything to make Jacqueline's ghost happy."

Benny got up and moved to stand near Grandfather. There were goose bumps along his arms. "I like gifts," he said in a shaky voice.

"So does the ghost," Miss Wolfson told Benny.

"Nonsense," Grandfather Alden cut in. "I've known this ghost story my whole life. There's no LaFonte ghost. Bad things happen to people sometimes—that's just the way life is. Good things happen too. It doesn't matter whether or not someone leaves presents in the cemetery."

"You're wrong. The ghost is real." A well-dressed woman in the back of the room stood up. She looked directly at Grandfather and asked, "Ever hear of Patricia Wilson? Patty didn't heed the warning, never left a gift, and she...disappeared!"

Several people in the room gasped.

"That's an old made-up rumor from the year after Jacqueline's death," Mr. Randy said from behind the cash register. "Patricia Wilson didn't disappear. My mother was a child back then and knew her."

Miss Wolfson pointed out Mr. Randy's mother in the photo taken in front of the old school house, a girl who looked to be about Violet's age.

"Mama knew Patty," Mr. Randy said in a booming voice that filled the café. "She told me that Patty left town on her own."

The woman turned to face Mr. Randy. "Believe what you want," she said, gathering her coat and scarf. "I won't risk having a year of bad luck. I'm going to put a gift at the cemetery tomorrow."

"What do you think?" Henry asked Jessie as people in the café began to discuss whether or not they were going to set out gifts for the ghost.

Jessie looked down at her notebook where she'd written Jacqueline LaFonte's name. On the next line, she wrote Patricia Wilson. And below that she drew a giant question mark.

"I'd like to learn more about the ghost," Jessie replied.

"And the gifts," Benny chimed in.

"We should go back to the cemetery,"

Henry suggested as a streak of lightning flashed across the sky outside the café.

"Can we go tomorrow?" Benny asked, patting his belly. "Now it really is dinnertime, and I'm starved! I'm extra brave when my tummy's full." He shivered again. "Ghosts. Yikes."

"The cemetery won't be so creepy in the daylight," Violet agreed.

Henry looked at the white lily and its reflection in the window glass. "We'll start ghost hunting tomorrow morning," he said.

Jessie quickly peeked over at Benny and added, "Right after breakfast."

"Perfect!" Benny grinned as they followed Grandfather to the car for the ride home.

CHAPTER 4

Gifts for Ghosts

"Isn't that Marcus Michelson?" Violet pointed toward the cemetery gate. She was walking with Jessie and her brothers. Marcus was coming straight toward them.

Jessie checked the time. They'd left home just after breakfast as planned. "He's out early," she remarked. "I wonder what he's doing here."

It wasn't raining anymore, but it was still cold. Marcus was wearing the same dark jacket as the evening before, but now his hood was down. In his hands he carried a cardboard box.

Benny was holding Watch's leash. When Watch saw Marcus, he tugged forward, pulling out of Benny's hand and running down the sidewalk.

Marcus wasn't paying attention and stumbled backward when Watch jumped up to greet him.

"Whoa!" Marcus said, dropping the box as Watch's leash tangled around his ankles. The lid on the box popped open and the contents spilled out. Two silver candlesticks lay on the sidewalk.

Henry rushed after the dog. "Sorry," he told Marcus.

"Watch just wants to make a new friend," Benny said. "He's a happy dog."

Henry unwound the leash then handed the end to Jessie.

"Are you all right?" Violet asked. Marcus seemed distracted. His eyes were darting around the area, not focusing on any one thing.

"I'm fine. I have to go." Marcus collected the candlesticks and set them carefully back into the box. "Now we'll see," he muttered to himself and then, without another word to the Aldens, he stomped through the cemetery gates.

Jessie watched him go.

"I think we should follow him," Henry suggested. "It looks like he's going to the LaFonte mausoleum."

"Do you think the candlesticks are a gift for the ghost?" Benny asked. "Do you think we should leave a gift too?"

"Grandfather said it's all made up," Henry reminded Benny. "No such thing as the LaFonte ghost."

"Lots of people believe the ghost is real." Benny lowered his voice and added, "And Patty Wilson disappeared..."

"She might have just left town," Jessie said.

"I agree with Benny," Violet admitted. "Until we know for sure what happened to Patty Wilson, I think we should leave a gift too."

"When we get home, I'll find a nice present for the ghost. Just in case she's real," Benny told Violet. "We don't want any bad luck."

The children entered the cemetery and stayed hidden in a grove of trees near the mausoleum. They watched as Marcus set down his box and removed the candlesticks. He carefully arranged them near a column then picked up the empty box and walked away.

"What do you think is going to happen to Marcus's gift?" Violet asked Henry.

"I think someone will come and get it," Henry replied. "Then we will know who is pretending to be the ghost."

"Isn't that stealing?" Jessie asked. "I mean, if someone invented a ghost to scare people into leaving food and silver and jewelry, then sneak in and collect it all—that seems like stealing to me."

"Right," Henry agreed. "The person who is doing this is definitely a thief."

"It's a ghost," Benny argued. "Not a thief."

"Where would the ghost put all those presents?" Henry asked.

"The ghost makes them magically disappear," Benny said.

"Magically disappear to where?" Henry pressed Benny to think about his answer. "People have been leaving things for the LaFonte ghost for seventy-four years. That's a lot of gifts."

"Not too many," Benny replied. "If I got presents on my birthday and at Christmas every year, I'd never run out of places to put all my gifts," Benny said. "They could all fit in the toy box and under the bed and in the closet." He smiled. "I have plenty of room for a hundred years of presents."

"You're funny," Henry said. "But ghosts don't have beds and closets. I think we need to stay here all day to see who's taking the gifts and prove there is no ghost."

"Maybe we can find out where the thief is putting the presents and return them to their owners," Jessie suggested.

"If we catch a person pretending to be a ghost, I *won't* believe in ghosts," Violet said very practically. "And if we see a real ghost, then I *will* believe in them."

"Ghosts. Yikes," Benny said as they searched for a better place to hide.

Jessie and Violet found a good spot in the old grove of trees where they could keep an eye on Marcus's candlesticks. Benny climbed up one of the trees for a better view.

Since they were going to be there all day, Henry ran home to take Watch back and pick up a pair of binoculars. He returned right away.

Hours later, Violet was bored. Besides Marcus, no one else had come to leave gifts at the mausoleum and Marcus's candlesticks were still sitting there. "I am beginning to think there's no ghost *and* no thief," she said. "Nothing interesting is going on."

"I'm cold," Jessie said. She'd left her hat at home and forgotten to ask Henry to pick it up when he went back.

Violet sneezed. "I'm cold too."

"And I'm hungry," Benny called down from the tree branch where he was camped out.

"I brought you lunch," Henry said, looking up at his brother.

"But that was *hours* ago," Benny said.

"And I brought snacks." Henry pointed at a trash bag filled with empty granola bar wrappers.

"We ran out ten minutes ago," Benny said with a sigh. "I ate them all."

"Hang in there," Henry told his siblings. "We can't give up yet. Something is going to happen—" Just then, he saw movement near the mausoleum. Henry put the binoculars to his eyes and adjusted the focus.

"What do you see?" Benny asked, sitting up straight and leaning forward. "Is it the ghost?"

"Or a person?" Jessie squinted in the direction Henry was looking.

Henry said, "I saw someone behind a tree. But just his or her arm—a black coat sleeve. Then it disappeared."

"A ghost," Benny said surely.

"A person," Jessie said, also certain.

Violet didn't take a side. She sneezed again instead.

"Get out!" A spooky voice called through the trees.

"Ghost!" Benny leapt down from the tree, knocking down Jessie.

"Person," Jessie said, getting up and turning him around to face Mrs. Radcliffe, the graveyard caretaker.

"Leave!" Mrs. Radcliffe pointed her long bony finger to the exit gate. "You are not welcome in my cemetery." Hunched over, wearing a black cloak, Mrs. Radcliffe looked like the wicked witch in the Hansel and Gretel story.

"We're watching for the LaFonte ghost," Henry said. "We're going to prove she's fake."

Mrs. Radcliffe shook her head. "Ghosts are supposed to scare people…" She muttered, "I've already chased someone else away. Now you all need to go too."

"Someone was hiding in the cemetery?" Violet asked. "Who?"

"I wish you'd all go away!" Mrs. Radcliffe said. "Everyone is leaving trash around, trampling on my grass, stepping on the flowers..." She didn't answer Violet's question. "I have to clean up. More work for me."

She led them to the gate and warned, "Stay outside the cemetery. I don't want you traipsing all over the place and climbing my trees! Leave my ghosts alone!"

"Ghosts?" Violet asked after Mrs. Radcliffe was gone. "Like more than one?"

"I don't think she really means that the cemetery is full of ghosts," Jessie said. "I think she's just trying to scare us away."

"It worked. I don't want to go back to the cemetery ever!" Benny gritted his teeth. "That lady is scarier than a ghost!"

"She's scary for sure," Violet agreed. "But how are we going to find out if there's a ghost *or* a thief without going back into the cemetery?"

Henry pointed to a tree outside the property. "Benny, can you climb up there and see if the candlesticks are still at the mausoleum?" he asked. Then to Violet, "Maybe we can investigate from here."

"I feel safer out here." Benny quickly

climbed the tree and surveyed the graveyard with Henry's binoculars. "Uh-oh. There's trouble," he reported. "You know how Marcus was the only one who left a gift today?"

"Yes," Jessie said, encouraging him to go on.

"Well, people must have been waiting till they were done with work—" Benny slid down the tree trunk. "Lots and lots of people are coming toward the cemetery now. And they're all carrying boxes."

Violet looked past Benny with the binoculars. "I see Vita. She's hiding in the bushes with her video camera." She handed the binoculars to Henry, saying, "If Mrs. Radcliffe spots her, she'll be chased out here with us."

Jessie shook her head. "Mrs. Radcliffe will never be able to chase everyone out of the cemetery."

"Let me see." Henry climbed up the tree to the branch where Benny had been. "There are a lot of people. I see Vita. There's the mausoleum. And—"

He put down the binoculars with a surprised look on his face.

"Marcus Michelson's candlesticks are gone!"

CHAPTER 5

Spooky Suspects and Creepy Clues

"How about this?" Benny held up one of Jessie's dolls from the toy bin in the boxcar clubhouse. She was dirty, had matted hair and a missing an arm, and wore only one shoe.

"I don't think you should give Beautiful Betsy to the ghost." Violet frowned. "She's not so beautiful anymore. That doll looks like she's had a lot of bad luck."

"There was no bad luck. Betsy was my favorite." Jessie defended her doll. "Grandfather gave her to me when we first came to live here. I used to take her everywhere with me."

"Still...Violet's right," Benny said with a frown. "The ghost would want something nicer." Benny put Betsy back in the toy box and searched around for something else. "How about this?" He held up one of Henry's old baseball gloves. It smelled bad. "Maybe not," he said, plugging his nose and tossing the glove back in the bin.

"You're not going to need a gift," Jessie assured Benny. "There's no ghost."

Jessie was at her desk, staring at the computer screen as a web page loaded.

Henry was standing over her shoulder. "There," he said. "Click on Jacqueline LaFonte's name." He scanned the source. "This is what the local newspaper said about her after she died."

Jessie read the page silently to herself then described what it said. "The whole article is about how Jacqueline was a kind woman who loved Greenfield." Jessie pinched her lips together. "I don't think Jacqueline LaFonte would haunt this town. It says here that she gave a lot of money to charity."

"Nice ghosts can be scary," Benny said.

"Jacqueline gave her money away," Henry said. "She didn't take anything from others." He glanced at the shiny plastic bead necklaces Benny was now holding. "It doesn't sound like she was the kind of person who'd want other people's jewelry and candlesticks."

"Then why do people leave gifts for her?" Violet asked. "There must be a reason."

"I don't know how it started," Jessie said as she flipped through a few more web sites. "I can't find anything about the beginning, but it says here that after her death people avoided her family because of the bad luck rumors. No one went to their businesses. The dress shop had to close. People were scared of the ghost and that made them scared of the LaFontes." She shook her head. "The family was run out of town. It's a shame."

Henry was using the Internet on his cell phone to help Jessie find out more information. "Hey, look here," he said, turning the phone screen around toward the others. "There's an old house on the hill behind the cemetery. It used to be their family home. No one's lived there for a long time. It's all run down now." Henry marked the web site photo. "We should check it out."

"I'll need a whole lot of snacks if I'm going to be brave enough to visit an abandoned house," Benny said, stretching as far as he could into the toy bin.

Violet gave him a playful push. Benny fell forward, toppling into the box. He was laughing as he dug himself out. "Maybe I should share my snacks with the ghost instead of giving her our old toys." He quickly changed his mind. "Nah." Benny ducked back into the bin. "I want the food. The ghost can have some toys."

Jessie opened her notebook and wrote a note to visit the old LaFonte house. Then she turned to a fresh page.

"Let's imagine we are catching a gift thief," she said. "Who are the suspects?"

"The ghost," Benny's muffled voice came

from the bottom of the toy chest. "The ghost is the first suspect."

Jessie didn't argue. She wrote it down.

"Marcus Michelson." Violet said. "He's new to town and has a black coat. We've seen him near the cemetery a couple times, which means he could be the one stealing the gifts. When we saw him at the café, he looked just like the spooky figure we'd seen near the mausoleum."

Jessie wrote his name down, along with all of Violet's reasons.

"But we also saw him putting his own gift out for the ghost," Henry said.

"Maybe I'm wrong," Violet admitted. "Until we know more, he should be a suspect."

"Okay. Let's find out what we can about Marcus," Jessie said, turning in her chair. She was rubbing her chin. Jessie did that when she was thinking really hard. "He could easily have set the flower on the café window."

Benny popped up. "That means the ghost was in the café! Yikes."

"The person *pretending* to be the ghost was

in the café," Henry corrected. He nodded toward Jessie's list. "Marcus Michelson is a suspect. But then, so is Miss Wolfson."

Jessie wrote down the historian's name, saying, "She was closest to the window when the lights went out. She had a black coat hanging on a hook. And it was wet. And she knows the most about the LaFonte ghost."

"Put Mrs. Radcliffe on the list too," Benny said, crawling out of the toy box with a handful of possible gifts.

"But she wasn't in the café," Violet argued.

"It doesn't matter if she was there or not. I think she's creepy," Benny replied, shaking his head.

"That's not a good reason to think someone is a thief," Henry said. "We can't just put her on the list because she looks like a witch and yells at children—"

"What if..." Jessie interrupted. "What if Mrs. Radcliffe invented the ghost to keep people out of the cemetery?"

"Her cloak *is* black," Violet said.

"She could have turned off the café lights,

sneaked in, placed the flower, and left before anyone noticed," Henry added.

"If she wants to scare people away, her plan's not working," Benny said, reminding them of the big crowd that was going to the cemetery with gifts.

"Let's put her on the suspect list," Henry told Jessie. "Just in case."

"Okay." Jessie wrote down Mrs. Radcliffe's name. "We have three possible gift-stealing thieves."

"And one ghost," Benny added. "Don't forget there is still the possibility the ghost is real."

"Right." Jessie checked the list. "Anyone else to consider?"

The room fell silent as everyone thought about who they'd seen lurking around the cemetery.

"Vita, maybe," Violet said. "Maybe she invented the ghost. She decided really fast to make a movie about it. An exciting scary movie could make her famous, right?"

"It's possible," Jessie said. "And she was

inside the café—"

"Wait!" Henry suddenly interrupted. "We have a problem." He breathed a heavy sigh and said, "A big problem."

"What?" everyone asked at the same time.

"The ghost was first spotted a year after Madame LaFonte died," Henry said. "That means whoever has been taking the gifts from the cemetery has been doing it for seventy-four years! No one on our list is old enough to have been there at the beginning."

"Oh." Jessie leaned back in her chair. "That is a problem," she admitted.

"A big problem," Violet echoed, tapping her foot.

"There's only one answer then." Benny found a roll of wrapping paper and began to wrap the toys he'd selected. "The LaFonte ghost is real!" He shuddered and added, "Yikes!"

CHAPTER 6

Patty Wilson

"We need to talk to the people on our suspect list," Jessie said.

Henry agreed. "Even though no one has been around for more than seventy-four years, maybe one of them still holds a clue to this ghost-thief mystery."

He called Vita Gupta.

Vita told him that she was headed to the cemetery to film Miss Wolfson talking about the legend of Jacqueline's ghost. Vita said they could meet there.

49

"I couldn't sleep last night," Jessie told the others as they walked to the cemetery.

"What did you do?" Benny asked. "Read? Watch TV? Din-eakfast?" He grinned at his new word. "That's the meal between dinner and breakfast."

"None of those," Jessie said with a small giggle. "I went to the boxcar and did some research. I found out what happened to Patty Wilson."

"Really?" Violet stepped up next to Jessie. "What'd you learn? I'm curious."

"So did she leave town on her own?" Henry asked. He dropped his voice to a spooky growl. "Or did the ghost get her?" Sneaking behind Violet, he tapped her on the shoulder.

"Augh!" Violet jumped.

They all laughed.

"This whole ghost thing still scares me a little," Violet admitted.

"And me a lot," Benny said, reaching into his jean pocket. He pulled out a squished granola bar in a crinkled plastic bag. "Want a snack for bravery?" He held the bar out to Violet.

"No, thanks," she said, eyeing the flattened honey-coated nut mixture.

"I'll eat it then." Benny peeled a piece of the bar away from the plastic. He tapped his other pocket. "I have another one in case I get scared later." Benny looked at Violet. "You can share it if you feel nervous."

Violet ruffled his brown hair and winked. "You're a good little brother."

Changing the subject back to Jessie's research, Henry asked, "What did you find out?"

Jessie handed Henry a page she'd printed from the Internet. It was an old newspaper article.

"Patty's sister was sick. She left town to help the family," Jessie said as Benny tugged hard on the cemetery gate to open it. "In those days, small newspapers used to run brief news articles about people in town. I'm guessing that no one thought to search other towns around Greenfield for information about her. I checked old newspaper records and found something from the town of Beacon Crest."

"I've never heard of Beacon Crest," Henry said.

"It doesn't exist now," Jessie told him. "When Silver Spring grew bigger, Beacon Crest became part of it. But seventy-five years ago, it was its own town."

"Clever, Jessie," Violet complimented her.

Jessie smiled. "Thanks."

Henry read the short newspaper notice out loud: "*Mrs. Laura Thompson was visited this week by her sister, Miss Patricia Wilson of Greenfield. Mrs. Thompson is at home, resting from her illness.*

"I knew it," Henry said as he led the way toward the mausoleum. "No ghostly bad luck."

"Or maybe it was the ghost's bad luck that got her sister sick," Benny suggested. "I mean, if she didn't leave Jacqueline LaFonte a gift, it's possible."

"Good point." Henry shrugged. "I guess I'm going to have to work harder to show you that the ghost doesn't exist."

"Try your best," Benny said. "Until you

prove it to me, I'm going to eat granola bars. Just in case you're wrong."

Violet wrapped her clean fingers around Benny's sticky ones. "We're protecting each other," she said with a wink.

"Yes, we are," Benny replied.

There was a big crowd at the LaFonte mausoleum. Miss Wolfson was in the center of the group, standing on a small step stool, talking in a loud voice.

"It all began one year after Jacqueline LaFonte died..." Miss Wolfson was saying.

"Looks like we didn't miss much," Henry whispered.

Marcus Michelson was near the front, hands in his black jacket pockets, listening intently.

Vita was there too. Her camera scanned the crowd and then focused on Miss Wolfson.

The Aldens stayed near the back of the crowd to listen.

"On the first anniversary of Madame LaFonte's death, Patricia Wilson found a lily near the LaFonte dress shop window.

Frightened, Patty ran down the street and found my mother at the bakery, working behind the counter. Patty was the assistant to Jacqueline at the dress shop. Patty said that before she died, Jacqueline announced that she planned to 'return' on her anniversary and that people should bring gifts to her grave or she'd bring bad luck."

A man near Marcus put his arm around his wife. She was holding a bouquet of flowers and a box of chocolates. Together they stepped forward and set the items on the steps of the mausoleum.

"My mother immediately left a gift. Patty meant to, she said she would, but she forgot." Miss Wolfson squinted her eyes and peered slowly across the faces of the audience. "Patricia Wilson disappeared before the three days passed."

"That's not exactly true," Jessie blurted out. All eyes turned to face her. She blushed. "Sorry. I didn't mean to interrupt," Jessie told Miss Wolfson. She reached into her coat pocket and took out the article. "Last night I discovered that Patty Wilson had been visiting her sick sister." She held up the page. "Exactly seventy-four years ago this time of year. Which means she left on her own. It wasn't a ghost that got her. She didn't really disappear."

Vita turned her camera on the Aldens.

Henry stood tall and said, "Maybe Patricia Wilson didn't tell anyone she was leaving. We think it was an emergency. Then she probably stayed in Beacon Crest and didn't come back."

"Look. There's more." Jessie held up a second sheet of paper and said, "I found more newspaper items about Patricia. She married and became Patricia Haverford and then she died in Silver City. Here's her death notice. Patty Wilson lived to be ninety-two years old. She had children and grandchildren."

People began to mutter and whisper to each other. It was as if no one had listened to Jessie.

"I heard about a man whose business went bankrupt," a lady reported. "And a girl who broke her arm."

"Well, I heard about a boy who got food poisoning. And one time, a man didn't leave a gift and a big storm came. A tree fell on the man's car."

Everyone had a bad luck story to tell about what had happened to someone who hadn't left Jacqueline LaFonte's ghost a present.

"That's all normal stuff," Henry said in a loud voice. "Bad stuff happens to everyone, but so does good stuff." That was exactly what Grandfather had told the children at the café when they saw the lily appear.

"It's the ghost's curse," someone said from deep inside the crowd.

Violet stood on her tiptoes but couldn't see who said it.

A nervous hush came over the people at the mausoleum. A little boy quickly walked to the pillars and set down a box of crayons near the name plaque. Three young girls put down home baked treats. A man set out candles and a woman carefully set down a pretty potted plant.

As the gifts piled up, Jessie turned to Henry,

Violet, and Benny. She waved the articles. "I don't understand," she said. "I have proof that Patricia Wilson didn't disappear, but no one believes it."

Henry frowned. "Let's go talk to Miss Wolfson. She's a historian. She has to believe the facts."

Because he was the smallest, Benny got through the crowd first.

Miss Wolfson was talking to Marcus Michelson. Vita was recording their conversation.

"I've changed my mind," Vita was telling Miss Wolfson. "Instead of the historical society film, I'm making a ghost documentary," Vita said. "I'm going to show the entire town coming out to leave gifts for the ghost. I've already talked to a big-time producer about making a spooky cemetery movie. She thinks I might become a famous director."

Miss Wolfson smiled and waved to the camera. "Hello, Hollywood," she said with a grin. Then Miss Wolfson sneezed. "Excuse

me," she told Vita. "I think I might be getting a cold."

Violet reached forward and handed Miss Wolfson a tissue. "Me too," she said with a sneeze.

Miss Wolfson took the tissue. "Thank you," she said. Then turned, "Jessie, can I see your pages?"

Jessie handed her the pages. Miss Wolfson took a quick glance before handing them back. "Good luck," she told Jessie.

"With what?" Violet asked. Miss Wolfson was acting strange.

"With convincing people that there is no ghost," Miss Wolfson said, putting her hands on her hips. "People believe what they want to believe. Remember my mom in the old school picture? Now, she's ninety-five years old. Just yesterday, she told me that even if Patty Wilson herself walked into the cemetery right now and declared she hadn't been cursed, no one would believe her. The ghost and the gifts and the story about bad luck are part of Greenfield's history. *Nothing* you do will change that." She added, "We all might as well make the best of it."

Bending down, Miss Wolfson told Benny, "Bring some toys. I'm sure the ghost would especially like to have a few stuffed animals and some board games."

Marcus Michelson's face became very red. "It's time for people to know the truth." He stomped his foot, then put the hood of his black coat over his head and shouted at Mrs. Wolfson, "For all the trouble that ghost has caused, those gifts should be mine!" With that, Marcus stormed out of the cemetery.

He left just in time because a few minutes later Mrs. Radcliffe appeared. She was carrying a broom and swinging it like a weapon. "Get out," she shrieked, sweeping at people's feet. "Out of my cemetery. Stay off the grass. Don't trample the flowers." People moved aside, but no one left. Finally in frustration, Mrs. Radcliffe muttered, "The LaFonte ghost isn't scary enough to keep people away. This cemetery needs a zombie!" With an angry huff, she stomped back to her office.

CHAPTER 7

Movie Magic

"Is there a zombie in Greenfield?" Benny asked at breakfast the next morning. "Mrs. Radcliffe said the cemetery needed a zombie." The children were sitting at the dining room table, which was laid out with bowls and spoons.

Violet came in from the kitchen carrying a box of cereal and a carton of milk. "Mrs. Radcliffe is just trying to frighten people away from the cemetery," Violet told Benny. "Ghosts maybe. Zombies...no way."

"A zombie would be scarier than a ghost," Benny said while pouring a bowl of crunchy flakes. "But know what would be even scarier?"

"What?" Jessie asked.

"Grrr," Benny snarled, showing his teeth. "A werewolf."

Jessie laughed. "Or a vampire." She covered her neck with two hands. "That would scare me."

"Mrs. Radcliffe scares me," Henry said with a wink. "I think she can chase people away from the cemetery all on her own!"

Everyone agreed.

"Good morning," Grandfather greeted the children as he brought his coffee cup and joined them at the table. "How's the ghost hunt going?"

"After last night, our suspects are all now more suspicious," Henry replied.

"It's day three," Jessie said. "The last day for people to bring gifts to the mausoleum."

"Or get bad luck." Benny trembled. "A whole year of bad luck."

Violet said to Grandfather, "If we don't

find a person acting like the ghost today, we might have to admit that the ghost is real."

"Or wait till next year to search around again," Henry said, shaking his head.

"So what's your plan for today?" Grandfather Alden asked as they finished their cereal. "Are you going back to the cemetery?"

"Maybe we should hide again and see if we can catch the person gathering the gifts," Henry suggested.

Jessie opened her notebook. "Remember when Henry found out about the old LaFonte house on the hill? I think we should go there," she said. "Maybe we can find a clue in the house."

Benny took his empty bowl and got up to go into the kitchen. "I'm going to need a lot of snacks if we're visiting a spooky haunted house." He patted his empty pockets. "Lots and lots of snacks."

"That reminds me," Jessie said, getting up from the table, "Watch is probably hungry too." She called to the dog. "Watch! Come here, Watch!"

Usually Watch came running at the sound of Jessie's voice. But not today.

"Watch!" she called again.

"Where's that dog?" Henry asked, going to search the bedrooms. "I bet he's sleeping, or—"

Just then Benny came running in from the kitchen. "Watch is gone!"

"What do you mean?" Violet asked, hurrying to Benny's side. She looked worried.

"When I came downstairs this morning, Watch wanted to go outside. So I tied his leash to the patio table. Now Watch is gone." Benny's eyes were wide. "I knew it! We should have brought a gift to the mass-o-lume."

"Mausoleum," Jessie corrected as she came back into the dining room. "There's no ghost."

"Then how do you explain this?" Benny held up Watch's leash. "Watch escaped. We have bad luck! We have bad, bad luck!"

Benny ran from the room and came back a second later, still in his pajamas and his morning hair sticking up to the sky. He was holding a big bag of toys. "Gifts for the ghost.

We have to deliver them right now so Watch
will come back. Hurry, Jessie. Hustle, Henry.
Come on, Violet." He slipped on his tennis
shoes. "Let's go to the..." he said it slowly to
be sure he said it right, "...mausoleum."

* * *

Watch wasn't at the cemetery. But plenty
of people were there, and the area around
the LaFonte mausoleum was piled high
with gifts.

Benny walked carefully through the crowd
until he reached one of the columns. He

set down his bag of toys and began to put them on the ground one at a time near the mausoleum steps.

"Wait!" Vita rushed to him. "Can you take them back and do it again? I want to record you for my movie."

Benny waited for his siblings to catch up. He asked Henry, "Is it bad luck to take them back? We've had enough bad luck already."

"I think it's all right," Henry assured Benny. "You really don't have to give gifts at all."

"Yes, we do! We have to save our dog!" Glancing down at his pajama bottoms, Benny told Vita, "We're kind of in a hurry to get these presents to the ghost." He asked, "Have you seen Watch? He's missing."

"That's terrible!" Vita said. "How about this? After I record you putting out the gifts, I'll help you find your dog. Filming will only take a couple minutes."

Benny agreed and took back his presents, putting them into the bag.

Vita asked him to move into the crowd

while she framed the shot. She wanted the old grove of trees behind him and the LaFonte house on the hill in the distance. Looking through her lens, Vita shouted, "Action!"

Benny wove his way through the people around the mausoleum toward the column again. He took the gifts out one by one and set them down. He had ten different wrapped packages. Then Benny turned to Vita's camera and said, "We don't want any bad luck. We just want our dog back."

Vita put down the lens. "That was perfect," she told Benny. "I'll quickly review it to make sure I got everything and that it's in focus. Then we can search for Watch."

Benny said, "I'm worried about our dog. Thanks for helping us."

"Thanks to you too," Vita replied. She switched the camera into playback mode.

"Did you know about the ghost story before you decided to make the movie?" Jessie asked Vita.

"No," Vita said. "I found out the same way you did. The lights went out at Randy's Café and then the lily appeared. That was the beginning." She looked at the small screen on her camera and rewound the part she'd filmed with Benny.

Violet took Jessie aside. "It doesn't sound like Vita is a suspect anymore."

"She didn't make up the ghost for her movie," Jessie agreed, taking out her notebook and crossing off Vita's name. "It was a coincidence that she was at the café that night."

Jessie closed the notebook and everyone huddled around Vita's camera to see the bit with Benny.

There he was, standing in the crowd. Then she moved out to the trees.

"Wait till I add spooky music," Vita said. "This is going to be awesome!"

From the trees, her lens panned up to the old house on the hill and then down to focus on Benny...

Suddenly, Vita gasped. She pressed the stop button on the camera and then pushed the footage back a few frames.

"What do you see?" Henry asked.

"Is it the ghost?" Benny shivered.

She zoomed in toward the house. "Look at this." Vita turned the tiny screen toward Henry and Jessie. Violet and Benny squeezed in to see. "There's something moving. There—" Vita's eyes went wide. "Near the front porch. By the steps."

"That's not a ghost!" Jessie gasped. She jumped up and started to run toward the house on the hill. "It's Watch!"

CHAPTER 8

Haunted House

"Don't worry." Benny untied the cord that held Watch to the splintered wooden stake in front of the LaFonte house. "We gave the ghost presents. Lots of presents. No more bad luck for the Aldens!"

"Watch didn't run away," Henry said, hooking Watch's leash to his collar. "Someone took him. On purpose."

"I wonder why," Jessie said, bending down to hug her dog. "Is someone trying to scare us away?"

Violet looked up at the old house and wrinkled her forehead. "Maybe whoever is pretending to be the ghost wanted us to come here."

"I don't think anyone wanted us to come here," Benny said. "In fact, I think we should leave. Fast as we can."

The LaFonte house was dark and dusty. When a gust of wind blew, the enormous house swayed. It was hard to imagine what it had been like when Jacqueline LaFonte lived there. It must have been beautiful, but now the windows were all broken. The fence had toppled down and was rotten. The garden was a field of weeds.

Jessie saw a rat scurry under the porch.

Violet glanced over her shoulder. "I want to go inside," she said.

"Come on, Violet." Vita was right behind her, camera held high. "We have a mystery to solve." She added, "This is going to be the best movie ever."

The children entered through a side door with broken hinges. The door led into a small kitchen area, where rusted appliances sat covered with silken spider webs and thick dust.

"I don't like it in here," Benny said, squeezing himself between Henry and Jessie. Benny took a granola bar out of his pocket but didn't eat it. He held it in his hand to give him courage.

The living room was in better shape than the kitchen, but barely. Antique furniture had been covered with sheets. The chandeliers were black with tarnish. The ceiling beams appeared sturdy, but birds had nested in the wide cracks.

"Okay," Violet said with a quick look around. "Nothing to see. No clues to who might be pretending to be a ghost." She crossed her arms and hugged herself. "No gifts. Let's go."

Henry insisted they take a peek in the dining room and a small parlor across the hall before they could leave. "No one would be foolish enough to try those stairs." He indicated that the only way to the second floor

was a narrow stairway with wilted boards and a broken handrail.

"A dead end. This is disappointing," Jessie said. "I hoped that the answer to who was playing the LaFonte ghost and what was happening to the gifts would be in this old house."

Henry headed to the front door. "We can leave this way." Reaching out, Henry said, "I'll unlock—"

The knob rattled.

"It's the ghost!" Benny exclaimed. "Yikes."

"We've gotta run." Violet was shaking.

When the knob rattled again, Henry jumped back, colliding with Violet and Jessie. Benny crashed into Vita, knocking the camera out of her hands. It skidded across the floor and hit a wall at the far end of the living room.

In the middle of the wall was a door that the children hadn't noticed during their quick look around. The door was covered with the same peeling wallpaper as the rest of the room. Had it not been for a small latch and the gap near the floor, the door would have completely blended into the wall.

"Whoa," Vita said, scooping up her camera. "What's this?" She reached out to tug the latch.

"Let's go back out through the kitchen," Violet said, hurrying in that direction. "I don't want to know what's in there."

"Just a quick look." Henry stepped next to Vita at the door. "It'll just take a second."

Violet cautiously stepped back into the room. "No such thing as ghosts," she told herself.

The door creaked as the hinges gave way and the door opened to reveal a closet.

Crash!

A vase fell off a tilted shelf and shattered on the living room floor.

Just then, the front door of the house opened with a bang. A figure wearing a black jacket, face obscured with a hood, stomped into the room.

It was too late to run. Vita slowly turned around and raised her camera lens to her eye. "If I'm going to face a ghost, I should film it," she said, breathing deeply. "A good director would never run away."

Henry, Violet, Jessie, and Benny stared at the figure. Watch growled.

Marcus Michelson pushed back his hood, revealing his face. "What are *you* doing here?" he demanded to know.

"I—" Vita was so nervous that she had a hard time forming words.

"We came to get our dog," Benny boldly told Marcus. "He was dog-napped."

"What are you doing here?" Henry asked.

"This is my family's house." Marcus dangled the door key. "And you are trespassing. I should call the police—" He stared at the Aldens and then at Vita. Behind her, the closet door was wide open and the broken vase lay on the floor.

Marcus walked forward with large steps. "Look. There are my candlesticks!" He gasped. Marcus took a flashlight out of his coat pocket and shone the beam inside the closet. The light glittered on his gift to the ghost.

The closet was deep. Henry and the others leaned forward to get a good look inside. Shelves ran floor to ceiling and they were packed full. Boxes sat on top of other boxes, piled high. Everything the children had seen left at the LaFonte mausoleum was in this closet. And there was plenty of room for today's final offerings.

"That's where my presents will go." Benny pointed to a big empty shelf near the back.

Henry turned toward Marcus. "You have a black coat like the one we saw in the cemetery. You were inside the café when the lily showed up. We saw you at the mausoleum. And we found the gifts in your family house." He scratched his forehead and ran a hand through his hair. "Everything seems to tell us that you are the thief. But I don't understand. Why would you steal your own candlesticks?"

"I promise you I didn't take my own candles," Marcus insisted. He looked over Henry's shoulder. "I've been to this old house a few times since I moved to town but never noticed that closet."

"It was hidden," Vita said. She shut the door to show him how the wallpaper perfectly matched up, making the door disappear into the wall.

"If you aren't the one pretending to be the ghost," Jessie said, opening her notebook and looking at Marcus's name on the suspect's page. "Who do you think it is?"

Vita was busy filming everything. She turned her camera to face the suspect. "What do you have to say, Mr. Michelson?"

"I don't—"

"Wait a second." Benny peered into Marcus's face. "Did you steal our dog?"

"I'm not the LaFonte ghost," Marcus said honestly. "But yes, I did take your dog."

CHAPTER 9

Who Is Greenfield's Ghost?

"You took our dog!" Benny stomped his feet. "That wasn't nice."

"I gave him water and food," Marcus assured Benny. "I did it because I wanted to get you out of the way." The college student looked from Benny to Jessie, to Violet and Henry. "I'm trying to find out who is pretending to be the ghost, and you children are always around, asking questions. You're ruining my investigation."

"We're searching for the same thing,"

Henry explained. "We could help each other."

"No," Marcus said. "I don't want help. I *need* to solve this mystery by myself."

"But we—" Henry began then changed his mind about what he was going to say. He looked to his siblings. "I just realized something important. Marcus is Madame LaFonte's grandson," Henry said.

"He is?" Violet asked. "How'd you know?"

"This is his family's house. He has the key," Henry explained. He asked Marcus, "You put out the candlesticks at the mausoleum so that you could see who took them, right?"

"Yes," Marcus said.

Jessie understood what had happened. She said, "When Mrs. Radcliffe said she chased someone else out of the cemetery that first night, it was Marcus. He was hiding to watch the candlesticks. Then, just like us, when he looked back from outside the cemetery— they were already gone."

"I missed seeing the thief and it's your fault. If I'd been the only one in the cemetery, Mrs. Radcliffe wouldn't have been so upset!"

Marcus said, "I have to find out who ruined my family name. I want to prove there is no bad luck. And I have to do it on my own."

"But we're good helpers—" Violet began.

"No!" Marcus growled at her. "I'm close to finding the truth. If you kids mess this up, I'll have to wait another year until Jacqueline LaFonte's next anniversary. I need to find out who started the rumor so that my parents and cousins can move back to town. I want to rebuild this house, open a business again, and start a fresh life here." He turned to Henry. "Please stop getting in my way. Let me find the thief."

"How do you know your grandmother is not really a ghost?" Benny asked.

"Grandmother LaFonte would never have stolen gifts. She was a kind and charitable person," Marcus said. "Did you know she gave money to the children's hospital?

"Did she give money to families with sick children too?" Jessie asked. She drew her eyebrows together as the answer became clear.

"Yes," Marcus said. "How'd you know?"

"Oh," Henry said, putting a hand on Jessie's shoulder. "I'm pretty sure that we just figured out who the ghost is. There's someone living in Greenfield today who gives money and volunteers at the children's hospital, just like your grandmother did."

"I get it!" Benny said. "I know who the ghost is."

"Who?" Violet sneezed. "I'm not sure who you are talking about." She sneezed again.

"Violet's cold is a clue too," Benny said. "The ghost also has a cold."

"I got the cold the first night—" Violet's eyes grew wide as she realized what Benny had figured out. "Whew. I'm glad there's no real ghost." Violet whispered the answer to Vita.

"Who is it?" Marcus Michelson asked, following the children outside. "I'm sorry," he apologized. "I've treated you all badly. I was wrong."

"You need to apologize to Watch," Benny said. "You dog-napped him."

Marcus got down on one knee to pet

Watch on the head. "Sorry, boy," he said. "I won't dog-nap any dog ever again."

Benny gave Marcus a long, hard look. "Promise?"

"Promise," Marcus agreed. He stood up and faced the children. "You all are very good detectives and I made a mistake thinking I could solve this mystery on my own." He went on, saying, "I really do need your help."

"Miss Wolfson is pretending she's the LaFonte ghost," Henry told him.

"I thought it might be her," Marcus said, thinking about it. "She has a black coat. And she knows a lot about the ghost and has been encouraging people to bring gifts to the mausoleum."

"She was also in the café when the flower appeared," Violet said.

"And her coat was wet," Jessie reminded everyone.

"When Violet sneezed, I remembered that Miss Wolfson also has a cold," Benny said. "I think that they both got sick being in the cemetery late at night in the rain."

"It seems possible, but Miss Wolfson couldn't have been the ghost for the last seventy-four years," Marcus said. "No way. She's not old enough."

"That is a problem," Violet admitted.

"Miss Wolfson is the ghost now..." Henry said.

"But," Jessie finished Henry's thought, "maybe she wasn't the original LaFonte ghost."

CHAPTER 10

Trick or Treat

Mrs. Arlene Wolfson was sitting in a rocking chair near the front window of the nursing home's recreation center. She was alone, knitting a purple scarf. Her gray hair shone in the sunlight and she had a smile on her face.

"Visitors!" Mrs. Wolfson exclaimed. Her smile broadened as the Aldens, Marcus, and Vita entered the room. "I love visitors."

"Hi," Benny said. He walked directly to her and asked, "Were you the first LaFonte ghost?"

Mrs. Wolfson nodded. "So, you found me out." She winked and dropped her voice to a whisper. "I'm ninety-five years old, you know. For a very long time I've hoped someone would figure it out. But no one ever came to see me." She rocked back and forth in her chair.

"I remembered that your daughter, Miss Wolfson, volunteers at the children's hospital," Jessie said. "And gives money to families with sick children."

"So did my grandmother," Marcus said, introducing himself.

"It looks like you've carried on with Jacqueline LaFonte's work," Violet said to Mrs. Wolfson.

"Yes. Yes. The hospital was important to Jacqueline. We've given a lot of money in her honor over the last seventy-four years," Mrs. Wolfson said, still knitting. "Every year, I collected the gifts and then sold them. Every cent went to charity. I also donated any food gifts and flowers to people who really needed them." She raised her head and looked at the children. "When I got too old, my daughter took over the job."

"I think what you've done is nice," Violet said. "But taking gifts from others is stealing." She frowned. "You're kind of a generous thief."

"I know," Mrs. Wolfson replied, clicking her tongue and shaking her head. "That's the part that I feel terrible about. I never wanted to steal from anyone. Really. It's strange how it all worked out. I never meant for this to happen."

"How did it begin?" Marcus wanted to

know. "I've spent my whole life wondering why people here are afraid of my family."

"I'm very sorry about that. Everything got out of control too quickly. The rumors spread like fire. No matter how hard I tried, I couldn't stop the flames." Mrs. Wolfson told the children to bring chairs over from a nearby table. "Let me tell you a story."

After asking for permission, Vita turned on her camera.

"It started as a joke," Mrs. Wolfson said. "After Jacqueline LaFonte died, we thought it would be funny to play a Halloween prank on the town. A little trick. Everyone used to do Halloween tricks back then. Much more fun than getting treats." She told Marcus, "Your grandmother had such a great sense of humor. She'd passed away the year before, but still, we thought she'd love to be part of the prank."

Marcus gave a small smile. "Yes. My mother told me how Grandma LaFonte used to play practical jokes on everyone. Once she put a live turtle in my mom's bathtub.

Another time she replaced all the flowers in the house with fake ones. Silly little things like that."

Mrs. Wolfson laughed. "Once, at the dress shop, she sewed a man's trouser legs together. He fell over when he tried to put them on. We laughed about it for days!"

"What did you do for the Halloween prank?" Violet asked.

"On the anniversary of her death, we put the lilies on her mausoleum, then set one in a shop in town. Patty made a big show of screaming in horror. She told everyone that before she died, Jacqueline said that anyone who didn't bring a present to her grave would have bad luck.

"The bad luck part was my idea," Mrs. Wolfson snickered. "It was very funny at first. Everyone was in a panic. Even people who didn't believe in ghosts or bad luck were bringing gifts—just in case." Her eyes clouded as she went on. "Patty and I thought it was the best joke ever played in Greenfield history. Better than when those boys put a cow in the mayor's office! Or the kids who dumped bubbles in the Main Street fountain." In a soft voice, she added, "We planned to give all the gifts back at the end of the three days."

"But Patty left town before it was over." Jessie knew that part of the story.

"Her sister got sick and needed help with her children. It was an emergency. Patty took the train the same day she heard the news." Mrs. Wolfson sighed. "Someone started a rumor that Patty had forgotten to leave a gift and disappeared." Her old shoulders sank. "Patty wrote me a letter that she wasn't coming back. Her sister needed her to stay. So, on my own, I went out to give back the gifts, but no one wanted them. They told me the ghost would harm them if they took back their presents."

Mrs. Wolfson stared out the window. "I tried and tried to explain. I talked until my voice hurt. No one wanted their things back. Finally, I gave up and donated the gifts to the hospital. I figured that Jacqueline would have liked hat."

"What happened next?" Marcus wanted to hear more.

"The following year, I didn't say anything about the ghost. No jokes. No pranks. No flowers. Nothing." Mrs. Wolfson raised her hands. "I couldn't believe it! The gifts piled up anyway." She shrugged. "I didn't know what to do. Again, I tried to give things back, but no one would take them. So once more, I donated them all."

"People started thinking my family brought bad luck." Marcus bit his bottom lip.

"It was bizarre. If a kid got the measles, they said it was the ghost. A dog got fleas. A man tripped on a curb..." Mrs. Wolfson said. "All anyone could talk about was the ghost's bad luck."

Violet let out a breath. She'd been holding it during the whole story. "This is terrible," she said. "Rumors can be very bad."

"After a few years, the LaFonte family moved away, and still the gifts kept coming on Jacqueline's anniversary. So I kept collecting them. I put them in the old empty house until

I could send them to the hospital or sell them for money to give to families who needed it."

Vita moved in for a tight shot of Mrs. Wolfson's face.

"When I moved here to the nursing home, my daughter took over." She glanced out the window. Henry could see the cemetery in the distance.

"You made something good come from something bad," Violet said. "You're not really a thief, are you?"

Mrs. Wolfson hesitated as she considered how to answer. "I don't know. Yes. No. Sort of—"

The door to the room opened. "Hello," Miss Wolfson greeted her mother's visitors as she stepped inside. "Did Mom tell you the truth?" she asked the Aldens.

"Yes," Jessie said. "It's a crazy story."

"I know!" Miss Wolfson took off her jacket and threw it over the back of an empty chair. "I'm so glad you children believe there's no ghost," she said. "I wish we could convince the rest of the town."

"There must be something we can do," Jessie said.

"Let's just tell people the history," Marcus said. "After we share the truth, my family will move back to Greenfield. It'll be over."

"It's not that easy," Violet told him. "Remember when Jessie brought proof that Patty Wilson didn't disappear because of the ghost's bad luck? She told everyone standing by the grave that Patty lived a long time. No one believed her."

"Just like no believed me all those years ago," Mrs. Wolfson said. "I'd have ended it seventy-four years ago if I could have."

"Well," Henry said, "we are going to have to *make* them believe us. No more bad luck. No more gifts."

Jessie thought about the words Mrs. Wolfson had used and said, "It's time to finally put out this fire."

"I definitely want the ghost story to end, but please don't forget about the hospital." Mrs. Wolfson was concerned. "The money, the flowers, and the food go to people who need it."

"Hmm," Marcus said. "That does make things complicated."

Vita lowered her camera. "Maybe..." she began. She turned the camera so that Henry could watch her whole movie from the beginning. "We can have a charity event for the hospital and get rid of the ghost at the same time."

"Leave it to us," Henry assured Miss Wolfson, Mrs. Wolfson, and Marcus. "We'll take care of everything!"

CHAPTER 11

Ghosts Gone?

The first annual Greenfield Halloween Charity Carnival took place in the cemetery parking lot.

"I knew there wasn't a real ghost," Benny said surely. "I knew it all along." He was standing in line for the Ferris wheel with Violet.

"So why are your pockets stuffed with granola bars?" Violet asked.

"In case I get hungry, of course," Benny said. He grinned and whispered, "Or in case we run into Mrs. Radcliffe. She still scares me." He shivered.

When Henry and Jessie went to the cemetery office to explain about the LaFonte ghost, they'd asked Mrs. Radcliffe if they could have the charity benefit in the cemetery.

"People are used to bringing gifts here," Henry had told her. "We simply want to take away the scary ghost part. They can donate whatever they want to the hospital."

Then Grandfather called Mrs. Wolfson at the nursing home and the younger Miss Wolfson at the historical society. He called the hospital to tell them about the charity carnival, and he called all his friends to come help.

Mrs. Wolfson and Miss Wolfson had set up the Greenfield Historical Society booth by the path to the cemetery. They entertained visitors with stories about Halloween pranks from Greenfield's town history.

From the top of the Ferris wheel, Benny could see that the place was packed. There were booths for games, a few fun rides, and in the center of it all stood the Children's Hospital LaFonte Donation Table.

"Bring your gifts here!" Jessie called out through a megaphone. There was a crowd of adults and children surrounding her. One by one, Jessie handed the gifts to Henry, who stood behind her.

"Drop off your donations to the children's hospital," Henry announced. He was piling the presents on a table.

Grandfather and Marcus Michelson were also standing at the table, wrapping the gifts in colored paper.

"Did you meet Marcus's mother?" Violet asked Benny as their swinging chair looped over the top of the wheel and began to sink back to earth.

"She's very nice," Benny said. "She makes dresses just like her mom did."

"I know!" Violet said. "She promised to make me something special. I can't wait. I picked out the fabric already. It's going to be purple to match the scarf Mrs. Wolfson made for me." She tightened the knitted scarf around her neck.

"I'm so glad we solved this mystery," Violet

said as the owner of the café opened the gate and let her and Benny off the ride. "It worked out for everyone. The rumors have stopped. The hospital gets presents. The LaFonte family can move back to town."

"Vita is showing her movie," Benny said. He checked the time. "We better hurry."

At the back of the parking lot a big white tent had been set up. The tent had long flaps to keep it dark inside.

Benny and Violet rushed to the front entrance.

"We're here," Violet told Vita.

"Just in time." Vita pointed to the line of people who'd come to see the movie. She told Violet where to stand. "Your job is to sell tickets. They cost a dollar. All the money will go to families with sick children."

Violet picked up a roll of tickets to sell. She was surprised when people gave her five or ten dollar bills and told her to keep the change.

"It's for charity," a woman said.

"It's good luck to give money to a good cause," a man said with a wink.

"Thanks!" Violet said, putting the money away and welcoming them into the tent.

Vita walked with Benny to another spot. "This is where you'll hand out popcorn," she told him. Smiling she added, "The popcorn was donated. It's free."

"Free food! My favorite kind." Benny stuffed a handful into his mouth.

"Save some for us, Benny," Henry said. He and Jessie entered the tent with Marcus and Grandfather. Behind them, the Wolfsons had also come to see the film.

"I hear I am going to be a celebrity," Mrs. Wolfson said.

"You sure are." A tall woman wearing a beautiful green suit stepped up to the group. "I'm Leanne Phuong. I came all the way from Hollywood to see Vita's movie. I'm a producer of ghost shows."

"You know there wasn't really ever a ghost," Miss Wolfson said, taking a bag of popcorn from Benny. "It was my mom. Then me."

"We know," Ms. Phuong assured her. "And we think it's a fabulous twist! A ghost story without a ghost. We are going to show this movie in film festivals all over the country."

Vita beamed. "Will you give all the ticket sales to local hospitals?" Vita asked. "That's an important part of the story."

"Of course!" Ms. Phuong agreed.

"My first movie." Vita was very happy.

"You better get started on a second film project," Henry told her.

"I've been thinking I'll make that one about the historical society next," Vita said. "The one I started before all this happened. There's a lot of history in Greenfield." She waved her hand outside the tent toward Main Street.

"Ohhh!" Benny was so excited he nearly dropped a bag of popcorn. "Please, Vita," he said. "I want to be the star of your movie!"

Everyone laughed.

The Aldens sat together in the front row of the tent theater. Suddenly, the lights flickered and went off.

"Oh no," Benny said, jumping up from his chair. "Could there be another ghost in the cemetery? Yikes." He took a granola bar out of his pocket and began to unwrap it. "Maybe this time it's a zombie! Double yikes."

Jessie put a hand on Benny's shoulder. "No ghost. No zombie. Not even a vampire. That was just Vita turning off the lights. The movie is starting."

A single lily sitting on a windowsill appeared on the screen.

"I don't believe in ghosts," Benny said firmly. Then he sat back to watch the movie.

Read a preview of...

MYSTERY OF THE FALLEN TREASURE

created by
Gertrude Chandler Warner

The Aldens visit Oregon and discover that Watch has what it takes to be a search and rescue dog. On his first day of training he finds something incredible in the woods: a backpack filled with expensive jewelry! When the children learn that it fell from a plane, the mystery gets stranger still. Whose backpack is it, and why did it fall from the sky?

CHAPTER 1

A New Adventure

"Look, that plane is flying awfully low!" Six-year old Benny Alden pointed out the window of the minivan. A small plane glided down past the mountains and disappeared in the distance.

"It's landing at the little Sunriver Airport," said Grandfather. "Lots of people have small planes there."

"I bet that plane is too small to hold all of us and our suitcases," Benny's ten-year-old sister, Violet, said. "Especially since we also have Watch with us!" She petted the wire-haired dog that sat next to her.

The Aldens had landed at the airport just before noon and rented the mini-van. Grandfather's friend Victor Gonzales had invited the family to spend a week in beautiful Sunriver in central Oregon. They had traveled across the country from Greenfield, Connecticut.

"Dogs are welcome in Sunriver," said Henry, Benny and Violet's older brother. He was reading from a brochure that he had downloaded from the Internet. Henry was fourteen and liked to look things up on the computer. "It says that dogs just have to be on a leash or be very well behaved."

Twelve-year-old Jessie reached past Violet to pet Watch. He turned to nuzzle her hand. "Watch is very well behaved, aren't you, Watch?"

Watch was really Jessie's dog, but Jessie was happy to share him with her sister and brothers. Jessie had found Watch in the woods. When their parents died, Jessie, Violet, Henry, and Benny had run away. They were supposed to live with their grandfather whom they had never met. They had heard that he was mean so they decided to hide from him. They discovered an abandoned boxcar in the woods and made it their home, which they shared with Watch. Their grandfather found them and they learned that he was not mean at all, but kind and loving. The Aldens became a family and Grandfather moved them all to his home in Greenfield. The boxcar was set up in the yard so the children could play there anytime they liked.

"The brochure also says that we can see the foothills of the Cascades from here," said Henry. "We are surrounded by wooded hills, mountains, and lakes."

Henry and the other children looked out the window at the scenery that surrounded them.

"What's a foothill?" asked Benny.

"It's a low hill at the base of a mountain or a mountain range," said Henry.

"They don't look like feet to me," said Benny.

Violet and Jessie laughed. "I bet they're called foothills because they are fun to walk on!" suggested Violet.

"That could be, Violet," said Henry. "Foothills are easier to hike up than mountains!"

"I hope we'll go hiking!" said Benny.

"I'm sure we will," said Jessie. "Watch will make sure that we do!"

"Grandfather, you'll want to turn right at the next street," Henry said. "Mr. Gonzales's house is just a few blocks away."

"Did you Google it on your cell phone?" Grandfather asked.

"Yes, I did," said Henry. The other children giggled. They knew that Henry loved high-tech devices.

They passed a small village with shops and restaurants and turned right.

"Are we there yet?" asked Benny. "I'm hungry—it must be past lunchtime!"

"We'll eat soon," promised Jessie. "We need to get our things put away first."

Grandfather steered the minivan into a circular driveway and pulled up next to a large log cabin. A woman waved at them from the front door and walked to the van as everyone got out. She had dark, curly hair and a friendly face.

"Greetings, Aldens!" she said as she helped grab suitcases.

"Oh my goodness, Marianella, you have grown up," said Grandfather. "Children, this is Victor's daughter, Marianella." Mr. Alden introduced Henry, Jessie, Violet, and Benny.

"We're pleased to meet you, Marianella," said Henry. The children all shook her hand.

"We're pleased to have you stay with us," said Marianella.

Watch sniffed at Marianella's hand and wagged his tail. "And this is Watch!" said Benny. "He smells something good on your hand."

"That's what he does when he thinks we have a treat for him," said Violet.

"That's funny and very smart of Watch," said Marianella. "Actually my father and I were just preparing lunch for everyone. Watch probably smells beef stew and cornbread!"

"Oooh! I love beef stew!" cried Benny. "And cornbread too."

"You love all food," laughed Jessie.

"I'll say hello to Victor," said Grandfather. He headed into the house.

Just then a huge brown-and-black dog charged up and sniffed excitedly at the Aldens.

"Goyo, how did you get loose?" asked Marianella. The dog ran to her side. "Don't worry, he is very friendly."

"We're very glad to meet you, Goyo," said Jessie. "Watch is also very friendly!"

Watch and Goyo sniffed noses and wagged their tails.

"I think lunch is ready," said Marianella. "Let's head inside and eat."

Benny was the first through the door. The rest of the family and Marianella carried in the baggage. After lunch the children helped wash and put away the dishes. Then Marianella showed them their room.

The large guest room had four bunk beds and plenty of space. The children put down the blankets they had brought from home for Watch. The dog settled on the blankets and Goyo joined him.

"This is almost like our boxcar," said Violet.

"Only this has real bunk beds instead of pine needle beds," said Benny.

Violet was looking at the photos on the wall. "Who is this?" she asked.

"Those are pictures of my sister, Adelita," said Marianella. "She's an airplane pilot."

"Wow, that's exciting," said Henry. "I

would love to learn how to fly an airplane."

"Yes, Adelita has always been the adventurous one," said Marianella. She studied the photos and sighed. "Father and I never know what she will do next. She has been acting strange lately."

Just then Goyo hopped up and came over to lick Marianella's hand. "Oh, you smart boy," she said, ruffling his head. "It's almost time to go, isn't it?"

"Where are you and Goyo going?" Benny asked.

"Oh, Benny, you're so nosy!" said Violet.

"It's okay," said Marianella. "We have a search-and-rescue training session in the foothills this afternoon."

"Goyo is a search-and-rescue dog?" Henry asked. "I've read about how dogs help find victims of disasters like earthquakes and avalanches. It sounds like dangerous work."

"It can be dangerous work, Henry," said Marianella. "And most SAR teams—as we're called—don't do it for money or glory."

"Wow," said Violet. "Have you and Goyo ever saved someone?"

"Goyo and I mostly look for lost hikers," said Marianella. "Sadly a lot of people get lost in this area. Some people don't tell anyone where they're going, and often they aren't prepared for an emergency. We have to act fast."

"If Goyo already knows how to search, how come you still practice?" Benny asked. He was eye level with the big dog. Goyo slipped over and licked Benny's face.

"We never stop practicing and training," said Marianella. "SAR requires handlers and their dogs to be in tip-top shape." Watch sniffed at Marianella and she bent down to pet him. "Say, let's see what kind of search dog Watch might be. If he can sniff out beef stew and cornbread, I bet he can sniff out a lost hiker!"

Marianella and the children headed to the huge, fenced-in backyard. "Okay, here's what we'll do," said Marianella. "Jessie and Violet can hold Watch and cover his eyes while Henry and I hide Benny."

Jessie and Violet carefully covered Watch's eyes with Violet's scarf as Marianella, Henry, and Benny raced to the end of the yard and

disappeared around the corner of a shed. Henry and Marianella returned without Benny.

"Okay, Benny is ready," said Marianella. "Watch already knows his scent, so just tell him to find Benny."

"Watch, find Benny!" said Jessie. She followed Watch as he ran around the yard. He sniffed the ground and sometimes stopped to sniff the air. He looked back at Jessie after a few minutes. "I think Watch is confused," said Jessie.

"Just encourage him," said Marianella. "Tell him to find Benny. Dogs often need encouragement to keep searching."

"Find Benny!" said Jessie. "You can do it! I know you can!" Watch circled back around the yard then stopped and sniffed again. He suddenly yipped and ran around the shed with Jessie following. He stopped at a truck that was parked there. Watch jumped up on the tailgate and barked.

"You found me!" yelled Benny as he stood up. The other children and Marianella joined them and helped Benny out of the truck bed.

"Watch did great, didn't he?" Benny said as

he hugged the dog close. The other children also petted and praised Watch.

"Yes, Watch did very well," said Marianella. "Hey, would you all like to come with me?" Marianella looked at the children crowded around their dog.

"To a real search-and-rescue training session?" Henry asked.

"Yes, you will be my special guests," said Marianella. "You can work with Watch on some object-searching skills. Plus we can always use new bodies to hide. Benny is a champ at playing the part of a lost hiker."

"As long as you don't forget where you hide me," said Benny.

"Who can forget you?" laughed Jessie. "You always make your presence known."

"Then it's settled. Let's go," said Marianella.

"This will be fun," said Violet. "I'll bring my camera. Maybe Watch will find something exciting!"

Marianella and the Alden children drove out of Sunriver and into the Cascade foothills close by. Marianella parked her jeep in a gravel parking lot surrounded by woods.

Benny noticed a bumper sticker on the

back window of the jeep. *"SAR means search and rescue!"* he read aloud. Benny was just learning to read. He liked to try to read signs everywhere he went.

"That's right, Benny," said Marianella. She led the children to a trail into the woods. "Hey, we're here and I brought some help!" she called.

"Over here," said a voice. They all walked over to a campsite where a man and a dog were standing. Marianella introduced the Alden children to Jason and his dog, Bounce.

"This is our dog, Watch," said Jessie. "He is just learning about search and rescue."

"And I know how to get lost!" added Benny.

Everyone laughed. Watch was off his leash and running around in the woods. Suddenly he started barking.

"What's the matter with Watch?" Benny asked.

"We need to go see!" said Jessie.

The children ran to catch up with their dog. Watch was standing in a small clearing and wagging his tail. A bright yellow backpack lay in front of him. It was muddy and partly open.

"It looks like a backpack, but what's inside?" asked Violet. Something in the backpack was glinting in the sun that streamed through the trees.

The children praised Watch and approached the bright yellow backpack carefully. Henry picked up a stick and poked at it then peered inside. Violet was right behind him. Her brown eyes opened wide when she saw the contents.

"It's filled with jewelry!" she cried. "Beautiful jewelry!"

THE BOXCAR CHILDREN SPOOKTACULAR SPECIAL
created by Gertrude Chandler Warner

Three spooky stories in one big book!

From ghosts to zombies to a haunting in their very own backyard, the Boxcar Children have plenty of spooktacular adventures in these three exciting mysteries.

978-0-8075-7605-2
US $9.99 paperback

THE ZOMBIE PROJECT
The story about the Winding River zombie is just an old legend. But Benny sees a strange figure lurching through the woods and thinks the zombie could be real!

THE MYSTERY OF THE HAUNTED BOXCAR
One night the Aldens see a mysterious light shining inside the boxcar where they once lived. Soon they discover spooky new clues to the old train car's past!

THE PUMPKIN HEAD MYSTERY
Every year the Aldens help out with the fun at a pumpkin farm. Can they find out why a ghost with a jack-o'-lantern head is haunting the hayrides?